First American edition, 1986.
Text copyright © 1986 by Judy Taylor
Illustrations copyright © 1986 by Peter Cross
First published in Great Britain by Walker Books Ltd.
Printed and bound in Italy by L.E.G.O., Vicenza.
Library of Congress Catalog Card Number: 85-31181
ISBN 0-399-21328-7
First impression

DUDLEY
GOES FLYING

PETER CROSS

Text by
JUDY TAYLOR

G.P. Putnam's Sons
New York

It was a cold night in Shadyhanger and there was the feeling of snow in the wind.

But Dudley was snug and warm. He had just woken up and was thinking about tea.

Dudley stoked up the fire and
put the kettle on to boil. Slowly
the room filled with smoke.

"I wonder if something is blocking the chimney?" thought Dudley. "I'd better go up and see."

Dudley took the elevator to
the top. The tree was swaying in
the wind. *Going up...*

Second
branch...

first
branch...

As Dudley stepped out he was
buffeted by the wind and large
leaves swirled about his head.
It was a dangerous night
to be out.

The dark clouds cleared from the moon. Dudley saw at once what was wrong. The chimney was blocked with leaves.

Dudley wrapped his tail around the branch and swung down over the chimney. He might just be able to reach if he stretched out at full mouse length.

Dudley swung backwards and
forwards, each swing bringing him
nearer to the chimney. One last
gust of wind and *bang!* he hit the
top of the chimney very hard.

The leaves flew free and the
smoke poured out but Dudley was
falling quickly through the cold
night air.

He grasped at a passing
leaf and slowed down with
an arm-pulling jerk.

Gently Dudley

and the

leaf

sailed

to the

ground.

Back inside his warm, snug
house Dudley found the kettle
boiling merrily. He made a large
pot of tea – and ate a specially
large piece of cake. Dudley began
to think that it might soon be time
for a nap.